SAVED at SEA

Mrs. O. F. Walton

abeka.
Pensacola, FL 32523-9100
an affiliate of PENSACOLA CHRISTIAN COLLEGE®

To the Reader

This fascinating story takes place on a little island off the coast of Great Britain around the year 1900. The lighthouse keepers on the island are from Scotland, and so several Scottish terms are used:

bonnie = pretty

wee = little, or tiny

lassie = a young girl (A *bonnie wee lassie* is a pretty little girl.)

lad = a boy or a young man

lass = a young woman

bairn (bern) = a child

tea = a light meal that English and Scottish people enjoy in the late afternoon, usually with a cup of hot tea

fortnight = a British term for two weeks

A dictionary will help you with other words you may not know.

Saved at Sea

Staff Credits
Author: Mrs. O. F. Walton
Editor: Marion Hedquist
Cover Designer: Michelle Johnson
Designer: Rob McLaughlin
Illustrators: Jason Atwell, Brian Jekel, Kyle Henry

© mcmxcvii Pensacola Christian College, Inc.   © mmxv   Educational Ventures, Inc.
All rights reserved. Printed in U.S.A.   2020 C07

No part of this publication may be reproduced or transmitted in any form or by any means, electronic or mechanical, including photocopy, recording, or any information storage and retrieval system, or by license from any collective or licensing body, without permission in writing from the publisher.

Contents

Chapter		Page
1	My Strange Home	2
2	The Flare at Sea	11
3	The Bundle Saved	18
4	Little Timpey	25
5	The Unclaimed Sunbeam	33
6	The Old Gentleman's Question	41
7	A Thick Fog	48
8	Waiting for the Boat	55
9	A Change in the Lighthouse	63
10	Our New Neighbor	71
11	On the Rock	78
12	The Sunbeam Claimed	86

CHAPTER 1

My Strange Home

It was a strange day, the day that I was born. The waves were beating against the lighthouse, and the wind was roaring and raging against everything. Had not the lighthouse been built very firmly into the strong, solid rock, it and all within it must have been swept into the deep, wild sea.

It was a terrible storm. My grandfather said he had never known such a storm since he came to live on the island more than forty years before.

Many ships went down in the storm that day, and many lives were lost. But in the very midst of it, when the wind was highest and the waves were strongest, and when the foam and the spray had completely covered the lighthouse windows, I, Alick Fergusson, was born.

I was born on a strange day, and I was born into a strange home. The lighthouse stood on an island, four miles distant from any land. The island was not very large; if you stood in the middle of it, you could see the sea all round you—that sea which was sometimes so blue and peaceful, and at other times was as black as ink and roaring and thundering on the rocky shores of the little island. At one side of the island on a steep rock overhanging the sea stood the lighthouse. Night after night, as soon as it began to grow dark, the lighthouse lamps were lighted.

I can remember as a child how I used to admire those lights. I would sit for hours watching them revolve and change in color. First there was a white light, then a blue one, then a red one, then a green one—then a white one again. And as the ships went by they always kept a lookout for our friendly lights, thereby avoiding the rocks of which they warned them.

My grandfather, old Sandy Fergusson, was one of the lighthouse men whose duty it was always to keep these lamps in order and to light them every night. He was a clever, active old man, and he did his work well and cheerfully. His great desire was to be able to hold his post till I should be able to take his place.

At the time when my story begins, I was nearly twelve years old and daily growing taller and stronger. My grandfather was very proud of me and said I should soon be a young man, and then he would get me appointed in his place to look after the lighthouse.

I was very fond of my strange home and would not have changed it for any other. Many people would have thought it dull, for we seldom saw a strange face, and the lighthouse men were only allowed to go on shore for a few hours once in every two months. But I was very happy and thought there was no place in the world like our little island.

Close to the tower of the lighthouse was the house in which my grandfather and I lived. It was not a large house, but it was a very pleasant one. All the windows looked out over the sea, and plenty of sharp sea air came in whenever they were opened. All the furniture in the house belonged to the lighthouse and had been there long before my grandfather came to live there. Our cups and saucers and plates had the name of the lighthouse on them in large gilt letters and a little picture of the lighthouse with the waves dashing round it. I used to think them very pretty when I was a boy.

We had not many neighbors. There was only one other house on the island, and it was built on the other side of the lighthouse tower. The house belonged to Mr. Millar, who shared the care of the lighthouse with my grandfather.

---

gilt: gold in color

Just outside the
two houses was a
court with a pump
in the middle
from which we got
our water. There
was a high wall
all round this
court which made
a little shelter
for us from the
stormy wind.

Beyond this court were
two gardens, divided by an iron railing.
The Millars' garden was very untidy and forlorn and filled with nettles, thistles, groundsel, and all kinds of weeds, for Mr. Millar did not care for gardening, and Mrs. Millar had six little children and had no time to look after it.

But our garden was the admiration of everyone who visited the island. My grandfather and I were at work in it every fine day

---

forlorn: in pitiful condition
groundsel: flowering plants

and took a pride in keeping it as neat as possible. Although it was so near the sea, our garden produced most beautiful vegetables and fruit, and the borders were filled with flowers—cabbage-roses, pansies, and wallflowers—

Saved at Sea

and many other hardy plants which were not afraid of the sea air.

Outside the garden was a good-sized field full of small hillocks, over which the wild rabbits and hares, with which the island abounded, were continually scampering. In this field were kept a cow and two goats to supply the two families with milk and butter. Beyond it was the rocky shore and a little pier built out into the sea.

On this pier I used to stand every Monday morning to watch for the steamer which called at the island once a week.

It was a great event to us when the steamer came. My grandfather and I and Mr. and Mrs. Millar and the children all came down to the shore to welcome it. This steamer brought our provisions for the week from a town some miles off and often brought a letter for Mr. Millar or a newspaper for my grandfather.

My grandfather did not get many letters, for there were not many people that he knew. He had lived on that lonely island the greater part of his life and had been quite shut out from the world. All his relatives were dead now, except my father, and what had become of him we did not know. I had never seen him, for he went away some time before I was born.

My father was a sailor, a fine, tall, strong young fellow, my grandfather used to say. He had brought my mother to the island and left her in my grandfather's care while he went on a voyage to Australia. He left in that same little steamer which called every Monday morning. My grandfather stood on the end of the pier as the steamer sailed out of sight, and my mother waved her handkerchief to him as long as any smoke was seen on the horizon. Grandfather has often told me how young and pretty she looked that summer morning. My father had promised to write soon, but no letter ever came. Mother went down to the pier every Monday morning for three long years to see if it had brought her any word from her sailor husband.

But after a time, her step became slower and her face paler, and at last she was too weak to go down the rocks to the pier when the steamer arrived on Monday morning. And soon after this I was left motherless.

From that day—the day on which my mother died—my grandfather became both father and mother to me. There was nothing he would not have done for me, and wherever he went and whatever he did, I was always by his side.

As I grew older, he taught me to read and write, for there was of course no school which I could attend. I also learned to help him trim the lamps and to work in the garden. Our life went on very evenly from day to day until I was about twelve years old. I used to wish sometimes that something new would happen to make a little change on the island. And at last a change came.

CHAPTER 2
The Flare at Sea

My grandfather and I were sitting at tea one dark November evening. We had been digging in the garden the whole morning, but in the afternoon it had become so wet and stormy that we had remained indoors.

We were sitting quietly at our tea, planning what we would do the next day, when the door suddenly opened and Mr. Millar put his head in.

Saved at Sea   **11**

"Sandy, quick!" he said. "Look here!"

My grandfather and I ran to the door and looked out over the sea. There, about three miles to the north of us, we saw a bright flare of light. It blazed up for a moment or two, lighting up the wild and stormy sky, and then it went out, and all was darkness again.

"What is it, Grandfather?" I asked. But he did not answer me.

"There's no time to lose, Jem," he said. "Out with the boat, my man!"

"It's an awful sea," said Millar, looking at the waves beating fiercely against the rocks.

"Never mind, Jem," said my grandfather. "We must do our best." So the two men went down to the shore, and I followed them.

"What is it, Grandfather?" I asked again.

"There's something wrong out there," said he, pointing to the place where we had seen the light. "That's the flare they always make when they're in danger and want help at once."

"Are you going to them, Grandfather?" I said.

"Yes, if we can get the boat out," he said. "Now, Jem, are you ready?"

"Let me go with you, Grandfather," I said. "I might be able to help."

"All right, my lad," he said. "We'll try if we can get her off."

I can see that scene with my mind's eye as though it were but yesterday—my grandfather and Mr. Millar straining every muscle to row the boat from land, while I clung on to one of the seats and tried in vain to steer her. I can see poor Mrs. Millar standing on the pier with her shawl over her head watching us, and two of her little girls clinging to her dress. I can see the waves, which seemed to be rising higher every moment, ready to beat our little boat to pieces. And I can see my grandfather's disappointed face, as, after many a fruitless attempt, he was obliged to give it up.

"It's no use, I'm afraid, Jem," he said at last. "We haven't hands enough to manage her."

So we got to shore as best we could and paced up and down the little pier. We could see nothing more. It was a very dark night, and all was perfect blackness over the sea.

---

obliged: forced

The lighthouse lamps were burning brightly; they had been lighted more than two hours before. It was Millar's turn to watch, so he went up to the tower, and my grandfather and I remained on the pier.

"Can nothing be done, Grandfather?"

"I'm afraid not, my lad. We can't make any way against such a sea as this; if it goes down a bit, we'll have another try at it."

But the sea did not go down. We walked up and down the pier almost in silence.

Presently a rocket shot up into the sky, evidently from the same place where we had seen the flare.

"There she is again, Alick! Poor things! I wonder how many of them there are."

"Can we do nothing at all?" I asked again.

"No, my lad," he said; "the sea's too much for us. It's a terrible night. It puts me in mind of the day you were born."

So the night wore away. We never thought of going to bed, but walked up and down the pier with our eyes fixed on the place where we had seen the lights. Every now and then for some hours rockets were sent up; then they ceased, and we saw nothing.

"They've got no more with them," said my grandfather. "Poor things! It's a terrible bad job."

"What's wrong with them, Grandfather?" I asked. "Are there rocks over there?"

"Yes, there's the Ainslie Crag just there; it's a nasty place, that—a very nasty place. Many a fine ship has been lost there!"

At last the day began to dawn; a faint gray light spread over the sea. We could distinguish now the masts of a ship in the far distance. "There she is, poor thing!" said my grandfather, pointing in the direction of the ship. "She's close on Ainslie Crag—I thought so!"

"The wind's gone down a bit now, hasn't it?" I asked.

"Yes, and the sea's a bit stiller just now," he said. "Give Jem a call, Alick."

Jem Millar hastened down to the pier with his arms full of rope.

"All right, Jem, my lad," said my grandfather. "Let's be off; I think we may manage it now."

Ainslie Crag (ānz/lē crăg): A crag is a steep, rugged rock that juts out from a land mass.
masts: tall poles that support the sails of a ship

So we jumped into the boat and put off from the pier. It was a fearful struggle with the winds and waves, and for a long time we seemed to make no way against them. Both the men were much exhausted, and Jem Millar seemed ready to give in.

"Cheer up, Jem, my lad," said my grandfather. "Think of all the poor fellows out there. Let's have one more try!"

So they made a mighty effort, and the pier was left a little way behind. Slowly, very slowly, we made that distance greater; slowly, very slowly, Mrs. Millar, who was standing on the shore, faded from our sight, and the masts of the ship in distress seemed to grow a little nearer. Yet the waves were still fearfully strong and appeared ready every moment to swallow up our little boat. Would my grandfather and Millar ever be able to hold on till they reached the ship, which was still more than two miles away?

"What's that?" I cried, as I caught sight of a dark object rising and falling with the waves.

"It's a boat, surely!" said my grandfather. "Look, Jem!"

CHAPTER 3

The Bundle Saved

It was a boat of which I had caught sight—a boat bottom upwards. A minute afterward it swept close past us, so near that we could almost touch it.

"They've lost their boat. Pull away, Jem!"

"Oh, Grandfather!" I said—and the wind was so high, I could only make him hear by shouting—"Grandfather, do you think the boat was full?"

"No," he said. "I think they've tried to put her off, and she's been swept away. Keep up, Jem!" For Jem Millar, who was not a strong man, seemed ready to give in.

We were now considerably more than halfway between the boat and the ship. It seemed as if those on board had caught sight of us, for another rocket went up. They had evidently kept one back, as a last hope, in case anyone should pass by.

As we drew nearer, we could see that it was a large ship, and we could distinguish many forms moving about on deck.

"Poor fellows! Poor fellows!" said my grandfather. "Pull away, Jem!"

Nearer and nearer we came to the ship, till at length we could see her quite distinctly. She had struck on Ainslie Crag, and her stern was under water, and the waves were beating wildly on her deck. We could see men clinging to the rigging which remained and holding on to the broken masts of the ship.

---

rigging: the chains and ropes that support the masts and sails of a ship

Saved at Sea **19**

I shall *never* forget that sight to my dying day! My grandfather and Jem Millar saw it, and they pulled on desperately.

And now we were so near to the vessel that had it not been for the storm which was raging, we could have spoken to those on board. Again and again we tried to come alongside the shattered ship but were swept away by the rush of the strong, resistless waves.

Several of the sailors came to the side of the ship and threw out a rope to us. It was long before we could catch it, but at last, as we were carried past it, I clutched it, and my grandfather immediately made it secure.

"Now!" he cried. "Steady, Jem! We shall save some of them yet!" and he pulled the boat as near as possible to the ship.

Oh, how my heart beat that moment, as I looked at the men and women all crowding toward the place where the rope was fastened!

"We can't take them all," said my grandfather anxiously. "We must cut the rope when we've got as many as the boat will carry."

I shuddered as I thought of those who would be left behind.

We had now come so close to the ship that the men on board would be able to watch their opportunity and jump into the boat whenever a great wave was past and there was a lull for a moment in the storm.

"Look out, Jem!" cried my grandfather. "Here's the first."

A man was standing by the rope with what appeared to be a bundle in his arms. The moment we came near, he seized his opportunity and threw it to us. My grandfather caught it.

"It's a child, Alick!" he said. "Put it down by you."

I put the bundle at my feet, and my grandfather cried, "Now another; quick, my lads!"

But at this moment Jem Millar seized his arm. "Sandy! Look out!" he almost shrieked.

My grandfather turned round. A mighty wave, bigger than any I had seen before, was coming toward us. In another moment we should have been dashed by its violence against the ship, and all would have perished.

My grandfather hastily let go the rope, and we just got out of the way of the ship before the wave reached us. And then came a noise, loud

Saved at Sea

as a terrible thunderclap, as the mighty wave dashed against Ainslie Crag. I could hardly breathe, so dreadful was the moment!

"Now back again for some more!" cried my grandfather, when the wave had passed.

We looked round, but the ship was gone! It had disappeared like a dream when one awakes—as if it had never been. That mighty wave had broken its back and shattered it into a thousand fragments. Nothing was to be seen of the ship or its crew but a few floating pieces of timber.

My grandfather and Millar pulled hastily to the spot, but it was some time before we could reach it, for we had been carried by the sea almost a mile away, and the storm seemed to be increasing in violence.

When at last we reached that terrible Ainslie Crag, we were too late to save a single life; we could not find one of those on board.

For some time we battled with the waves, unwilling to relinquish all hope of saving some of them. But we found at last that it was of no use, and we were obliged to return.

All had perished except the child lying at my feet. I stooped down to look at it, and could hear that it was crying, but it was so tightly tied up in a blanket that I could not see it nor release it.

We had to strain every nerve to reach the lighthouse. It was not so hard returning as going, for the wind was in our favor, but the sea was still strong, and we were often in great danger. I kept my eyes fixed on the lighthouse lamps and steered the boat as straight as I could. Oh, how thankful we were to see those friendly lights growing nearer! And at last the pier came in sight, and Mrs. Millar was still standing there watching us.

"Have you got none of them?" she said as we came up the steps.

"Nothing but a child," said my grandfather sadly. "Only one small child, that's all. Well, we did our very best, Jem, my lad."

Jem was following my grandfather with the oars over his shoulder. I came last with that little bundle in my arms.

The child had stopped crying now and seemed to be asleep, it was so still. Mrs. Millar

Saved at Sea

wanted to take it from me and to undo the blanket, but my grandfather said, "Bide your time, Mary; bring the child into the house, my lass; it's bitter cold out here."

So we all went up through the field and through our garden and the court. The blanket was tightly fastened round the child, except at the top, where room had been left for it to breathe, and I could just see a little nose and two closed eyes as I peeped in at the opening.

The bundle was a good weight, and before I reached the house I was glad of Mrs. Millar's help to carry it. We came into our little kitchen, and Mrs. Millar took the child on her knee and unfastened the blanket.

"Bless her," she said, as her tears fell fast; "it's a little girl!"

"Aye," said my grandfather, "so it is; it's a bonnie wee lassie!"

---

bide: to wait; to stay
Aye (ī): yes

CHAPTER 4
Little Timpey

I do not think I have ever seen a prettier face than that child's. She had light brown hair, and round rosy cheeks, and the bluest of blue eyes.

She awoke as we were looking at her, and seeing herself among strangers, she cried bitterly.

"Poor little thing!" said Mrs. Millar. "She wants her mother."

"Mam—ma! Mam—ma!" cried the little girl, as she caught the word.

Mrs. Millar fairly broke down at this and sobbed and cried as much as the child.

"Come, my lass," said her husband; "cheer up! You'll make her worse if you take on so."

But Mrs. Millar could do nothing but cry. "Just think if it was our Polly!" was all that she could say. "Oh, Jem, just think if it was our Polly that was calling for me!"

My grandfather took the child from her and put her on my knee. "Now, Mary," he said, "get us a bit of fire and something to eat; there's a good woman! The child's cold and hungry, and we're much about the same ourselves."

Mrs. Millar bustled about the house and soon lighted a blazing fire; then she ran in next door to see if her children, whom she had left with a little servant girl, were all right, and she brought back with her some cold meat for our breakfast.

I sat down on a stool before the fire with the child on my knee. She seemed to be about two years old, a strong, healthy little thing. She had stopped crying now and did not seem to be afraid of me; but whenever any of the others came near, she hid her face in my shoulder.

Mrs. Millar brought her a bowl of bread and milk, and she let me feed her.

She seemed very weary and sleepy, as if she could hardly keep her eyes open. "Poor wee lassie!" said my grandfather. "I expect they pulled her out of bed to bring her on deck. Won't you put her to bed?"

"Yes," said Mrs. Millar, "I'll put her in our Polly's bed; she'll sleep there quite nice, she will."

But the child clung to me, and she cried so loudly when Mrs. Millar tried to take her that my grandfather said:

"I wouldn't take her away, poor motherless lamb; she takes kindly to Alick; let her bide here."

So we made up a little bed for her on the sofa, and Mrs. Millar brought one of little Polly's nightgowns and undressed and washed her and put her to bed.

The child was still very shy of all of them but me. She seemed to have taken to me from

Saved at Sea

the first, and when she was put into her little bed, she held out her tiny hand to me and said, "Handie, Timpey's handie."

"What does she say? Bless her!" said Mrs. Millar, for it was almost the first time that the child had spoken.

"She wants me to hold her little hand," I said. "Timpey's little hand. Timpey must be her name!"

"I never heard of such a name," said Mrs. Millar. "Timpey, did you say? What do they call you, darling?" she said to the child.

But the little blue eyes were closing wearily, and very soon the child was asleep. I still held that tiny hand in mine as I sat beside her; I was afraid of waking her by putting it down.

"I wonder who she is," said Mrs. Millar in a whisper as she folded up her little clothes. "She *has* beautiful things on, to be sure! She has been well taken care of, anyhow! Stop, here's something written on the little petticoat; can you make it out, Alick?"

I laid down the little hand very carefully and took the tiny petticoat to the window.

"Yes," I said, "this will be her name. Here's *Villiers* written on it."

"Dear me!" said Mrs. Millar. "Yes, that will be her name. Dear me, dear me; to think of her poor father and mother at the bottom of that dreadful sea! Just think if it was our Polly!" And then Mrs. Millar cried so much again that she was obliged to go home and finish her cry with her little Polly clasped tightly in her arms.

My grandfather was very worn out with all he had done during the night and went upstairs to bed. I sat watching the little sleeping child. I felt as if I could not leave her.

She slept very quietly and peacefully. Poor little pet! How little she knows what has happened, I thought; and my tears came fast and fell on the little fat hand which was lying on the pillow. But after a few minutes I leaned my head against the sofa and fell fast asleep. I had had no sleep the night before and was quite worn out.

I was awakened, some hours after, by someone pulling my hair and a little voice calling in my ear, "Up! Up, boy! Up! Up!"

I looked up and saw a little roguish face looking at me—the merriest, brightest little face you can imagine.

"Up, up, boy, please!" she said again, in a coaxing voice.

So I lifted up my head, and she climbed out of her little bed on the sofa onto my knee.

"Put shoes on, boy," she said, holding out her little bare toes.

I put on her shoes and stockings, and then Mrs. Millar came in and dressed her.

It was a lovely afternoon; the storm had ceased while we had been asleep, and the sun was shining brightly. I got the dinner ready, and the child watched me and ran backward and forward, up and down the kitchen. She seemed quite at home now and very happy.

My grandfather was asleep, so I did not wake him. Mrs. Millar brought in some broth she had made for the child, and we dined together. I wanted to feed her as I had done the night before, but she said:

---

roguish (rō′gĭsh): playfully mischievous

"Timpey have 'poon, please!" and took the spoon from me and fed herself so prettily, I could not help watching her.

"God bless her, poor little thing!" said Mrs. Millar.

"God bless 'ou," said the child. The words were evidently familiar to her.

"She must have heard her mother say so," said Mrs. Millar, in a choking voice.

When we had finished dinner, the child slipped down from her stool and ran to the sofa. Here she found my grandfather's hat, which she put on her head, and my scarf, which she hung round her neck. Then she marched to the door and said, "By-by, by-by; Timpey go by-by."

"Take her out a bit, Alick," said Mrs. Millar. "Stop a minute, though; I'll fetch her Polly's hood." So, to her great delight, we dressed her in Polly's hood and put a warm shawl round her, and I took her out.

Oh, how she ran and jumped and played in the garden! I never saw such a merry little thing. Now she was picking up stones, now she was gathering daisies (day-days, she called them), now she was running down the path and calling to me to catch her. She was never still a single instant!

But every now and then, as I was playing with her, I looked across the sea to Ainslie Crag. The sea had not gone down much, though the wind had ceased, and I saw the waves still dashing wildly upon the rocks.

And I thought of what lay beneath them, of the shattered ship, and of the child's mother. "Oh, if she only knew!" I thought, as I listened to her merry laugh, which made me feel more like crying than her tears had done.

CHAPTER 5

The Unclaimed Sunbeam

My grandfather and Jem Millar were sitting over the fire in the little watch-room in the lighthouse tower, and I sat beside them with the child on my knee. I had found an old picture-book for her, and she was turning over the leaves and making her funny little remarks on the pictures.

"Well, Sandy," said Millar, "what shall we do with her?"

"*Do* with her?" said my grandfather, stroking her little fair head. "We'll keep her! Won't we, little lassie?"

"Yes," said the child, looking up and nodding her head as if she understood all about it.

"We ought to look up some of her relatives, it seems to me," said Jem. "She's sure to have some somewhere."

"And how are we to find them out?" asked my grandfather.

"Oh, the captain can soon find out for us what ship is missing, and we can send a line to the owners; they'll know who the passengers were."

"Well," said my grandfather, "maybe you're right, Jem; we'll see what they say. But for my part, if those that care for the child are at the bottom of that sea, I hope no one else will come and take her away from us."

"If I hadn't so many of them at home—" began Millar.

"Oh, yes, my lad, I know that," said my grandfather, interrupting him; "but your house is full enough already. Let the wee lassie come to Alick and me. She'll be a nice little bit of company for us, and Mary will see to her clothes and such like, I know."

"Yes, that she will," said her husband. "I do declare she has been crying about that child the best part of the day! She has indeed!"

My grandfather followed Jem's advice and told Capt. Sayers, when he came in the steamer the next Monday, the whole story of the shipwreck and asked him to find out for him the name and address of the owners of the vessel.

Oh, how I hoped that no one would come to claim my little darling! She became dearer to me every day, and I felt as if it would break my heart to part with her. Every night, after Mrs. Millar had undressed her, she knelt beside me in her little white nightgown to "talk to God," as she called praying. She had evidently learned a little prayer from her mother, for the first night she began of her own accord:

> Jesus, Eppy, hear me.

I could not think at first what it was that she was saying, but Mrs. Millar said she had

Saved at Sea

learned the hymn when she was a little girl, and she wrote out the first verse for me. And every night afterward I let the child repeat it after me.

> Jesus, tender Shepherd, hear me,
> > Bless Thy little lamb tonight,
> Through the darkness be Thou near me,
> > Keep me safe till morning light.

I thought I should like her always to say the prayer her mother had taught her. I never prayed myself—my grandfather had never taught me. I wondered if my mother would have taught me if she had lived. I thought she would.

I knew very little in those days of the Bible. My grandfather did not care for it and never read it.

He had a large Bible, but it was always laid on the top of the chest of drawers as a kind of ornament, and unless I took it down to look at the curious old pictures inside, it was never opened.

Sunday on the island was just the same as any other day. My grandfather worked in the garden or read the newspaper, just the same as usual, and I rambled about the rocks or did my lessons or worked in the house, as I did every other day in the week. We had no church or chapel to go to, and nothing happened to mark the day.

I often think now of that dreadful morning when we went across the stormy sea to that sinking ship. If our boat had capsized then, if we had been lost, what would have become of our souls? It is a very solemn thought, and I cannot be too thankful to God for sparing us both a little longer. My grandfather was a kindhearted, good-tempered, honest old man; but I know now that that is not enough to open the door of Heaven. Jesus is the only way

---

capsized: overturned

there, and my grandfather knew little of, and cared nothing for, *Him.*

Little Timpey became my constant companion, indoors and outdoors. She was rather shy of the little Millars, for they were noisy and rough in their play, but she clung to me and never wanted to leave me. Day by day she learned new words, and she came out with such odd little remarks of her own that she made us all laugh. Her great pleasure was to get hold of a book and pick out the different letters of the alphabet, which, although she could hardly talk, she knew quite perfectly.

Dear little pet! I can see her now, sitting at my feet on a large rock by the seashore and calling me every minute to look at *A,* or *B,* or *D,* or *S.* And so by her pretty ways she crept into all our hearts, and we quite dreaded the answer coming to the letter my grandfather had written to the owners of the *Victory,* which, we found, was the name of the lost ship.

It was a very wet day, the Monday that the answer came. I had been waiting some time on the pier and was wet through before the steamer arrived. Capt. Sayers handed me the letter before anything else, and I ran up with it to my grandfather at once. I could not wait until our provisions and supplies were brought on shore.

Little Timpey was sitting on a stool at my grandfather's feet, winding a long piece of tape round and round her little finger. She ran to me as I came in and held up her face to be kissed.

What if this letter should say she was to leave us and go back by the steamer! I drew a long breath as my grandfather opened it.

It was a very civil letter from the owners of the ship, thanking us for all we had done to save the unhappy crew and passengers, but saying they knew nothing of the child or her belongings, as no one of the name of Villiers had taken a cabin and there was no sailor on board by that name. But they said they would make further inquiries in Calcutta, from which port the vessel had sailed. Meanwhile they

---

civil: polite
Calcutta: a seaport in India

begged my grandfather to take charge of the child and assured him he should be handsomely rewarded for his trouble.

"That's right!" I said, when he had finished reading it. "Then she hasn't to go yet!"

"No," said my grandfather; "poor wee lassie! We can't spare her yet. I don't want any of their rewards, Alick, not I! That's reward enough for me," he said, as he lifted up the child to kiss his wrinkled forehead.

CHAPTER 6
The Old Gentleman's Question

The next Monday morning Timpey and I went down together to the pier to await the arrival of the steamer. She had brought a doll with her which Mrs. Millar had given her and of which she was very proud.

Capt. Sayers sent for me as soon as the steamer came up to the pier to tell me that two gentlemen had come to see my grandfather. I

Saved at Sea **41**

held the child's hand very tightly in mine, for I felt sure they had come for her.

The gentlemen came up the steps a minute or two afterward. One of them was a middle-aged man, with a very clever face, I thought. He told me he had come to see Mr. Alexander Fergusson and asked me if I could direct him which way to go to the house.

"Yes, sir," I said; "Mr. Fergusson is my grandfather." So we went up toward the lighthouse, Timpey and I walking first to lead the way, and the gentlemen following. The other gentleman was quite old and had white hair, gold spectacles, and a pleasant, kind face.

Timpey could not walk very fast, and she kept running first to one side and then to another to gather flowers or pick up stones until I took her in my arms and carried her.

"Is that your little sister?" asked the old gentleman.

"No, sir," I said; "this is the little girl who was on board the *Victory*."

"Dear me! dear me!" said both gentlemen at once. "Let me look at her," said the old man, arranging his spectacles.

But Timpey was frightened, and she clung to me and began to cry. "Never mind, never mind," said the old gentleman kindly; "we'll make friends with one another by-and-by."

By this time we had reached the house, and the middle-aged gentleman introduced himself as Mr. Septimus Forster, one of the owners of the lost vessel, and said that he and his father-in-law, Mr. Davis, had come to hear all the particulars that my grandfather could give them with regard to the shipwreck.

My grandfather begged them to sit down and told me to prepare breakfast for them at once. They were very pleasant gentlemen, both of them, and were very kind to my grandfather. Mr. Forster wanted to make him a handsome present for what he had done, but my grandfather would not take it. They talked much of little Timpey, and I kept stopping to listen as I was setting out the cups and saucers. They had heard nothing more of her relatives, and they said it was a very strange thing that no such name as Villiers was to be found on the list of passengers on board. They offered to take her away with them till some relative was found, but my grandfather begged to keep her. The gentlemen, seeing how happy and well cared for the child was, gladly consented.

After breakfast Mr. Forster said he should like to see the lighthouse, so my grandfather went up to the top of the tower with him and showed him with great pride all that was to be seen there. Old Mr. Davis was tired and stayed behind with little Timpey and me.

"This is a strong house, my lad," he said, when the others had gone.

"Yes, sir," I said, "it ought to be strong; the wind is fearful here sometimes."

"What sort of a foundation has it?" said the old man, tapping the floor with his stick.

"Oh, it's all rock, sir," I answered, "solid rock; our house and the lighthouse tower are built into the rock; they would never stand if they weren't."

"And are *you* on the Rock, my lad?" said Mr. Davis, looking at me through his spectacles.

"I beg your pardon, sir," I said, for I thought I had not heard him rightly.

"Are *you* on the Rock?" he repeated.

"On the rock, sir? Oh, yes," I said, thinking he could not have understood what I said before. "All these buildings are built into the rock, or the wind and sea would carry them away."

"But *you*," said the old gentleman again, "are *you* on the Rock?"

"I don't quite understand you, sir," I said.

"Never mind," he said; "I'll ask your grandfather when he comes down." So I sat still, wondering what he could mean, and almost thinking he must have gone out of his mind.

As soon as my grandfather returned, he put the same question to him; and my grandfather answered it as I had done, by assuring him how firmly and strongly the lighthouse and its surroundings were built into the solid rock.

"And you yourself," said Mr. Davis, "how long have you been on the Rock?"

"I, sir?" said my grandfather. "I suppose you mean how long have I lived here; forty years, sir—forty years come the twelfth of next month I've lived on this rock."

"And how much longer do you expect to live here?" said the old gentleman.

"Oh, I don't know, sir," said my grandfather. "As long as I live, I suppose. Alick, here, will take my place by-and-by; he's a fine, strong boy, is Alick, sir."

"And where will you live when you leave the island?" asked Mr. Davis.

"Oh, I never mean to leave it," said my grandfather; "not till I die, sir."

"And *then;* where will you live *then?*"

"Oh, I don't know, sir," said my grandfather. "In Heaven, I suppose. But, dear me, I'm not going there just yet," he said, as if he did not like the turn the conversation was taking.

"Would you mind answering me one more question?" said old Mr. Davis. "Would you kindly tell me *why* you think you'll go to Heaven? You won't mind my asking you, will you?"

"Oh, dear, no," said my grandfather, "not at all, sir. Well, sir, you see, I've never done anybody any harm, and God is very merciful, and so I've no doubt it will be all right at last."

"Why, my dear friend," said the old gentleman, "I thought you said you were on the

Rock. You're not on the Rock at all; you're on the sand!" He was going to add more, when one of Capt. Sayers's men ran up to say the steamer was ready to start, and would they kindly come at once, as it was late already. So the two gentlemen jumped up and prepared hastily to go down to the beach.

But as old Mr. Davis took leave of my grandfather, he said earnestly:

"My friend, you are building on the sand; you are indeed, and it won't stand the storm; no, it won't stand the storm!" He had no time to say more, because the sailor hastened him away.

I followed them down to the pier and stood there watching the steamer preparing to start.

There was a little delay after the gentlemen went on board, and I saw Mr. Davis sit down on a seat on deck, take out his pocketbook, and write something on one of the leaves. Then he tore the leaf out and gave it to one of the sailors to hand to me as I stood on the pier, and in another moment the steamer had started.

Saved at Sea **47**

CHAPTER 7
A Thick Fog

That little piece of paper which was given me that day, I have it still, put among my greatest treasures. There was not much written on it, only two lines of a hymn:

>On Christ, the solid Rock, I stand;
>All other ground is sinking sand.

I walked slowly up to the house thinking. My grandfather was out with Jem Millar, so I did not show him the paper then, but I read the lines many times over as I was playing with little Timpey, and I wondered very much what they meant.

In the evening my grandfather and Jem Millar generally sat together over the fire in the little watch-room upstairs, and I used to take little Timpey up there until it was time for her to go to bed. She liked climbing up the stone steps in the lighthouse tower. She used to call out, "Up! up! up!" as she went along until she reached the top step, and then she would run into the watch-room with a merry laugh.

As we went in this evening, my grandfather and Jem were talking together of the visit of the two gentlemen. "I can't think what the old man meant about the rock," my grandfather was saying. "I couldn't make head or tail of it, Jem; could you, my lad?"

"Look there, Grandfather," I said, as I handed him the little piece of paper and told him how I had got it.

"Well, to be sure!" said my grandfather. "So he gave you this, did he?" and he read aloud:

> On Christ, the solid Rock, I stand;
> All other ground is sinking sand.

"Well, now, Jem, what does he mean? He kept on saying to me, 'You're on the sand, my friend; you're on the sand, and it won't stand the storm!' What do you make of it, Jem? Did you hear him, my lad?"

"Yes," said Jem thoughtfully, "and it has set me thinking, Sandy; I know what he meant well enough."

"And pray what may that be?"

"He meant we can't get to Heaven except we come to Christ; we can't get there no other way. That's just what it means, Sandy!"

"Do you mean to tell me," said my grandfather, "that I shan't get to Heaven if I do my best?"

"No, it won't do, Sandy; there's only one way to Heaven; I know that well enough."

"Dear me, Jem!" said my grandfather. "I never heard you talk like that before."

"No," said Jem, "I've forgotten all about it since I came to the island. I had a good mother years ago; I ought to have done better than I have done."

He said no more, but he was very silent all that evening. Grandfather read his newspaper aloud and talked on all manner of subjects, but Jem Millar's thoughts seemed far away.

The next day was his day for going on shore. My grandfather and Jem took it in turns—the last Friday in every month; it was the only time they were allowed to leave the island. When it was my grandfather's turn, I generally went with him, and I much enjoyed getting a little change. But whichever of them went, it was a great day with us on the island, for they bought any little things that we might be needing for our houses or gardens and did any business that had to be done on shore.

We all went down to the pier to see Jem Millar start; and as I was helping him to get on board some empty sacks and some other things he had to take with him, he said to me, in an undertone:

"Alick, my lad, keep that bit of paper; it's all true what that old gentleman said. I've been thinking of it ever since; and, Alick," he whispered, "I believe I *am* on the Rock now."

He said no more, but arranged his oars, and in a minute more he was off. But as he rowed away, I heard him singing softly to himself:

On Christ, the solid Rock, I stand;
All other ground is sinking sand.

We watched the boat out of sight and then went home, wishing that it was evening and that Jem was back again with all the things that we had asked him to get for us.

That was a very gloomy afternoon. A thick fog came over the sea and gradually closed us in so that we could hardly see a step before us on the beach.

Little Timpey began to cough, so I took her indoors and amused her there with a picture-book. It grew so dark that my grandfather lighted the lighthouse lamps soon after dinner. There was a dull, yellow light over everything.

I never remember a gloomier afternoon; and as evening came on, the fog grew denser, till at length we could see nothing outside the windows.

It was no use looking out for Jem's return, for we could not see the sea, much less any boat upon it. So we stayed indoors, and my grandfather sat by the fire smoking his pipe.

"I thought Jem would have been here before now," he said at length, as I was putting out the cups and saucers for tea.

"Oh, he'll come before we've finished tea, I think, Grandfather," I answered. "I wonder what sort of a spade he'll have got for us."

When tea was over, the door opened suddenly, and we looked up, expecting to see Jem enter with our purchases. But it was not Jem; it was his wife.

"Sandy," she said, "what time do you make it? My clock's stopped!"

"Twenty minutes past six," said my grandfather, looking at his watch.

"Past six!" she repeated. "Why, Jem's very late!"

"Yes," said my grandfather; "I'll go down to the pier and have a look out."

But he came back soon, saying it was impossible to see anything. The fog was so thick, he was almost afraid of walking over the pier. "But he's bound to be in at seven," he said (for that was the hour the lighthouse men were required to be on the island again), "so he'll soon be up now."

Saved at Sea   53

The clock moved on, and still Jem Millar did not come. I saw Mrs. Millar running to her door every now and then with her baby in her arms to look down the garden path. But no one came.

At last the clock struck seven.

"I never knew him do such a thing before!" said my grandfather, as he rose to go down to the pier once more.

CHAPTER 8

Waiting for the Boat

Poor Mrs. Millar went out of her house and followed my grandfather down to the pier. I waited indoors with little Timpey, straining my ears to listen for the sound of their footsteps coming back again.

But the clock struck half-past seven, and still no sound was to be heard. I could wait no

Saved at Sea   **55**

longer; I wrapped the child in a shawl and carried her into the Millars' house, leaving her under the care of Mrs. Millar's little servant. And then I ran down through the thick, smothering fog to the pier.

My grandfather was standing there with Mrs. Millar. When I came close to them, he was saying, "Cheer up, Mary, my lass; he's all right; he's only waiting till this mist has cleared away a bit. You go home, and I'll tell you as soon as ever I hear his boat coming. Why, you're wet through, woman; you'll get your death of cold!"

Her thin calico dress was soaked with the damp in the air, and she was shivering and looked as white as a sheet. At first she would not be persuaded to leave the pier; but, as time went on and it grew darker and colder, she consented to do as my grandfather told her, and he promised he would send me up to the lighthouse to tell her as soon as Jem arrived.

When she was gone, my grandfather said, "Alick, there's something wrong with Jem, depend upon it. I didn't like to tell her so, poor soul! If we only had the boat, I would go out a little and see."

We walked up and down the pier and stopped every now and then to listen if we could hear the sound of oars in the distance, for we should not be able to see the boat till it was close upon us, so dense had the fog become.

"Dear me," my grandfather kept saying anxiously, "I wish he would come!"

My thoughts went back to the bright, sunny morning when Jem Millar had started, and we had heard him singing, as he went, those two lines of the hymn:

> On Christ, the solid Rock, I stand;
> All other ground is sinking sand.

The time passed on. Would he never come? We grew more and more anxious. Mrs. Millar's servant girl came running down to say her mistress wanted to know if we could hear anything yet.

"No," my grandfather said, "nothing yet, my lass; but it can't be long now."

"Missis is so poorly," said the girl; "I think she's got a cold: she shakes all over, and she keeps fretting so."

"Poor soul! Well, perhaps it's better so."

"Whatever do you mean, Grandfather?" I asked.

"Why, if aught's amiss, she won't be so taken aback as if she wasn't afraid; and if Jem's all right, why, she'll only be the better pleased."

The girl went back, and we still waited on the pier. "Grandfather," I said at length, "I think I hear a boat."

It was a very still night; we stood and listened. At first my grandfather said he heard nothing, but at length he distinguished, as I did, the regular plash—plash—plash—of oars in the distance.

"Yes, it *is* a boat," said my grandfather.

I was hastening to leave the pier and run up to the house to tell Mrs. Millar, but my grandfather laid his hand on my shoulder.

"Wait a bit, Alick, my lad," he said. "Let us hear what it is first; maybe it isn't Jem, after all!"

---

aught's amiss: anything's wrong
at length: after a while

"But it's coming here, Grandfather; I can hear it better now."

"Yes," he said, "it's coming here." But he still kept his hand on my shoulder.

The boat had been a long way off when we first heard it, for it was many minutes before the sound of the oars seemed to become much more distinct. But it came nearer, and nearer, and nearer. Yes, the boat was evidently making for the island.

At last it came so near that my grandfather called out from the end of the pier.

"Hollo, Jem! You're late, my lad!"

Saved at Sea

"Hollo!" said a voice from the boat; but it wasn't Jem's voice. "Whereabouts is your land place?" said the voice. "It's so thick, I can't see."

"Why, Jem isn't there, Grandfather!" I said, catching hold of his arm.

"No," said my grandfather; "I knew there was something wrong with the lad."

He called out to the man in the boat the direction in which he was to row, and then he and I went down the steps together and waited for the boat to come up.

There were four men in the boat. They were sailors—strangers to me. One of them, the one whose voice we had heard, got out to speak to my grandfather.

"Something's wrong," said my grandfather before he could begin; "something's wrong with that poor lad."

"Yes," said the man, "we've got him here"; and he pointed to the boat.

A cold shudder passed over me as he said this, and I caught sight of something lying at the men's feet in the bottom of the boat.

"What's wrong with him? Has he had an accident? Is he much hurt?"

"He's dead," said the man solemnly.

"Oh, dear!" said my grandfather in a choking voice. "However shall we tell his wife? However shall we tell poor Mary?"

"How did it happen?" I asked at length, as soon as I could speak.

"He was getting a sack of flour on board, over yonder," said one of the men in the boat, "and it was awful thick and foggy. He missed his footing on the plank and fell in; that's how it happened!"

"Yes," said another man, "and it seems he couldn't swim, and there was no boat nigh at hand to help him. Joe Malcolmson was there and saw him fall in; but before he could call any of us, it was all over with him. We got him out at last, but he was quite gone. We fetched a doctor and took him into a house near and rubbed him and did all we could, but it wasn't of no good at all! Shall we bring him in?"

"Wait a bit," said my grandfather. "We must tell that poor girl first. Which of you will go and tell her?"

The men looked at each other and did not speak. At last one of them, who knew my

Saved at Sea **61**

grandfather a little, said, "You'd better tell her, Sandy; she knows you, and she'll bear it better than from strangers. We'll wait here till you come back, and then we can bring him in."

"Well," said my grandfather with a groan, "I'll go then! Come with me, Alick, my lad," said he, turning to me; "but, no, perhaps I'd better go by myself."

So he went very slowly up toward the lighthouse, and I remained behind with the four men on the shore and that silent form lying in the bottom of the boat.

I was much frightened and felt as if it were all a very terrible dream, and as if I should soon wake up to find it had all passed away.

CHAPTER 9

A Change in the Lighthouse

It seemed a long time before my grandfather came back, and then he only said in a low voice, "You can bring him now, my lads; she knows about it now."

And so the mournful little procession moved on, through the field and garden and court, to the Millars' house, my grandfather and I following.

I shall never forget that night, nor the strange, solemn feeling I had then.

Saved at Sea

Mrs. Millar was very ill; the shock had been too much for her. The men went back in the boat to bring a doctor to the island to see her, and the doctor sent them back again to bring a nurse. He said he was afraid she would have an attack of brain fever, and he thought her very ill indeed.

My grandfather and I sat in the Millars' house all night, for the nurse did not arrive until early in the morning. The six children were fast asleep in their little beds. I went to look at them once, to see if my little Timpey was all right; she was lying in little Polly's bed, their tiny hands fast clasped together as they slept. The tears came fast into my eyes as I thought that they both had lost a father, and yet neither of them knew anything of their loss!

When the nurse arrived, my grandfather and I went home. But we could not sleep; we lighted the kitchen fire and sat over it in silence for a long time.

Then my grandfather said: "Alick, my lad, it has given me such a turn as I haven't had for many a day. It might have been *me,* Alick; it might just as well have been *me!*"

I put my hand in his and grasped it very tightly as he said this. "Yes," he said again, "it might have been me; and if it had, I wonder where I would be now?"

I didn't speak, and he went on.

"I wonder where Jem is now, poor fellow; I've been thinking of that all night, ever since I saw him lying there in the bottom of that boat."

So I told him of what Jem Millar had said to me the last time I had seen him.

" 'On the Rock!' " said my grandfather. "Did he say he was 'on the Rock'? Dear me! I wish I could say as much, Alick, my lad."

"Can't you and I come as he came, Grandfather?" I said. "Can't we come and build on the Rock, too?"

"Well," said my grandfather, "I wish we could, my lad. I begin to see what he meant, and what the old gentleman meant, too. He said, 'You're on the sand, my friend; you're on the sand, and it won't stand the storm; no, it won't stand the storm!' I've just had those words in my ears all the time we were sitting over there by Mrs. Millar. But, dear me, I

Saved at Sea **65**

don't know how to get on the Rock; I don't indeed."

The whole of the next week, poor Mrs. Millar lay between life and death. At first the doctor gave no hope whatever of her recovery; but after a time she grew a little better, and he began to speak more encouragingly. I spent my time with the poor children and hardly left them a moment, doing all I could to keep them quietly happy that they might not disturb their mother.

One sorrowful day my grandfather and I were absent for several hours from the lighthouse, for we went ashore to follow poor Jem Millar to the grave. His poor wife was unconscious and knew nothing of what was going on.

When after some weeks the fever left her, she was still very weak and unfit for work. But there was much to be done, and she had no time to sit still, for a new man had been appointed to take her husband's place, and he was to come into the house at the beginning of the month.

We felt very dull and sad the day that the Millars went away. We went down to the pier with them and saw them on board the steamer—Mrs. Millar, the six little children, and the servant-girl, all dressed in mourning, and all of them crying. They were going to Mrs. Millar's home, far away in the north of Scotland, where her old father and mother were still living.

The island seemed very lonely and desolate when they were gone. If it had not been for our little sunbeam, as my grandfather called her, I do not know what we should have done. Every day we loved her more, and what we dreaded most was that a letter would arrive some Monday morning to tell us that she must go away from us.

"Dear me, Alick," my grandfather would often say, "how little you and I thought that stormy night what a little treasure we had got wrapped up in that funny little bundle!"

The child was growing fast; the fresh sea air did her great good, and every day she became prettier and more intelligent.

---

mourning: black clothes worn as a sign of grief for one who has died

We were very curious to know who was appointed in Jem Millar's place; but we were not able to find out even what his name was. Capt. Sayers said that he did not know anything about it, and the gentlemen who came over once or twice to see about the house being repaired and put in order for the newcomer were very silent on the subject and seemed to think us very inquisitive if we asked any questions. Of course, our comfort depended very much upon who our neighbor was, for he and

---

inquisitive: asking more questions than necessary; prying my grandfather would be constantly together, and we should have no one else to speak to.

My grandfather was very anxious that we should give the man a welcome to the island and make him comfortable on his first arrival. So we set to work as soon as the Millars were gone to dig up the untidy garden belonging to the next house and make it as neat and pretty as we could for the newcomers.

"I wonder how many of them there will be," I said as we were at work in their garden.

"Maybe only just the man," said my grandfather. "When I came here first, I was a young unmarried man, Alick. But we shall soon know all about him; he'll be here next Monday morning, they say."

"It's a wonder he hasn't been over before," I said, "to see the house and the island. I wonder what he'll think of it?"

"He'll be strange at first, poor fellow," said my grandfather, "but we'll give him a bit of a welcome. Have a nice bit of breakfast ready for him, Alick, my lad, and for his wife and bairns too, if he has any—hot coffee and cakes, and a bit of meat, and anything else you like; they'll be glad of it after crossing over here."

So we made our little preparations and waited very anxiously indeed for Monday's steamer.

CHAPTER 10
Our New Neighbor

Monday morning came and found us standing on the pier as usual awaiting the arrival of the steamer.

We were very anxious indeed to see our new neighbors. A nice little breakfast for four or five people was set out in our little kitchen, and I had gathered a large bunch of dahlias from our garden to make the table look cheerful and bright. All was ready, and in due time the steamer came puffing up toward the pier. We saw a man, who we felt sure must be the new lighthouse man, standing on the deck, talking to Capt. Sayers.

"I don't see a wife," said my grandfather.

"Nor any children," said I, as I held little Timpey up that she might see the steamer.

"Puff, puff, puff," she said as it came up, and then turned round and laughed merrily.

The steamer came up to the landing place, and my grandfather and I went down the steps to meet Capt. Sayers and the stranger.

"Here's your new neighbor, Sandy," said the captain. "Will you show him the way to his house while I see to your goods?"

"Welcome to the island," said my grandfather, grasping his hand.

He was a tall, strongly built man, very sunburned and weather-beaten.

"Thank you," said the man, looking at me all the time. "It *is* pleasant to have a welcome."

"That's my grandson Alick," said my grandfather, putting his hand on my shoulder.

"Your grandson," repeated the man, looking earnestly at me; "your grandson—indeed!"

"And now come along," said my grandfather, "and get a bit of something to eat; we've got a cup of coffee all ready for you at home, and you'll be right welcome, I assure you."

"That's very kind of you," said the stranger.

We were walking up now toward the house, and the man did not seem much inclined to talk. I fancied once that I saw a tear in his eye, but I thought I must have been mistaken. What could he have to cry about? I little knew all that was passing through his mind.

"By the bye," said my grandfather, turning round suddenly upon him, "what's your name? We've never heard it yet!"

The man did not answer, and my grandfather looked at him in astonishment. "Have you got no name?" he said. "Or have you objections to folks knowing what your name is?"

"Father!" said the man, taking hold of my grandfather's hand. "Don't you know your own lad?"

"Why, it's my David! Alick, look Alick, that's your father; it is indeed!"

Saved at Sea

And then my grandfather fairly broke down and sobbed like a child, while my father grasped him tightly with one hand and put the other on my shoulder.

"I wouldn't let them tell you," he said; "I made them promise not to tell you till I could do it myself. I heard of Jem Millar's death as soon as I arrived in England, and I wrote off and applied for the place at once. I told them I was your son, Father, and they gave it to me at once, as soon as they heard where I had been all these years."

"And where have you been, David, never to send us a line all the time?"

"Well, it's a long story," said my father; "let's come in, and I'll tell you all about it."

So we went in together, and my father still looked at me. "He's very like *her*, Father," he said, in a husky voice.

I knew he meant my mother!

"Then you heard about poor Alice?" said my grandfather.

"Yes," he said; "it was a very curious thing. A man from these parts happened to be on board the vessel I came home in, and he told me all about it. I felt as if I had no heart left in me, when I heard she was gone. I had just been thinking all the time how glad she would be to see me."

Then my grandfather told him all he could about my poor mother—how she had longed to hear from him and how, as week after week and month after month went by and no news came, she had gradually become weaker and weaker. All this and much more he told him; and whenever he stopped, my father always wanted to hear more, so that it was not until we were sitting over the watch-room fire in the evening that my father began to tell us his story.

He had been shipwrecked on the coast of China. The ship had gone to pieces not far from shore, and he and three other men had

Saved at Sea

escaped safely to land. As soon as they
stepped on shore, a crowd of Chinese gathered
round them with anything but friendly faces.
They were taken prisoners and carried before
some man who seemed to be the governor of
that part of the country. He asked them a
great many questions, but they did not understand a word of what he said and, of course,
could not answer him.

For some days my father and the other
men were very uncertain what their fate
would be, for the Chinese at that time were
exceedingly jealous of any foreigner landing
on their shore. However, one day they were
brought out of the wooden house in which
they had been imprisoned and taken on a
long journey of some two hundred miles into
the interior of the country. And here it was
that my poor father had been all those years
when we thought him dead. He was not unkindly treated, and he taught the half-civilized
people there many things which they did not
know and which they were very glad to learn.
But both by day and night he was carefully
watched lest he should make his escape, and

he never found a single opportunity of getting away from them. Of course, there were no mail and no railways in that remote place, and he was quite shut out from the world. Of what was going on at home he knew as little as if he had been living on the moon.

Slowly and drearily eleven long years passed away, and then one morning they were suddenly told that they were to be sent down to the coast and put on board a ship bound for England. They told my father that there had been a war and that one of the conditions of peace was that they should give up all the foreigners in their country whom they were holding as prisoners.

"Well, David, my lad," said my grandfather, when he had finished his strange story, "it's almost like getting you back from the dead to have you in the old home again!"

CHAPTER 11
On the Rock

About a fortnight after my father arrived, we were surprised one Monday morning by another visit from old Mr. Davis. His son-in-law had asked him to come to tell my grandfather that he had received a letter with regard to the little girl who was saved from the *Victory*. So he told my father and me as we stood on the pier; and all the way to the house I was wondering what the letter could be.

Timpey was running by my side, her little hand in mine, and I could not bear to think how lonely we should be when she was gone.

"Why, it's surely Mr. Davis," said my grandfather, as he rose to meet the old gentleman.

"Yes," said he, "it is Mr. Davis; and I suppose you can guess what I've come for."

"Not to take our little sunbeam, sir," said my grandfather, taking Timpey in his arms. "You never mean to say you're going to take her away?"

"Wait a bit," said the old gentleman, sitting down and fumbling in his pocket; "wait until you've heard this letter, and then see what you think about her going."

And he began to read as follows:

My Dear Sir:

I am almost overpowered with joy by the news received by telegram an hour ago. We had heard of the loss of the VICTORY, *and were mourning for our little darling as being among the number of those drowned. Her mother has been quite crushed by her loss and has been dangerously ill ever since the sad intelligence reached us.*

Need I tell you what our feelings were when we suddenly heard that our dear child was alive, and well, and happy!

We shall sail by the next steamer for England to claim our little darling. My wife is hardly strong enough to travel this week, or we should come at once. A thousand thanks to the brave men who saved our little girl. I shall hope soon to be able to thank them myself. My heart is too full to write much today.

Our child was traveling home under the care of a friend, as we wished her to leave India before the hot weather set in, and I was not able to leave for two months. This accounts for the name Villiers not being on the list of passengers on board the VICTORY.

Thanking you most sincerely for all your efforts to let us know of our child's safety,

I remain, yours very truly,

        EDWARD VILLIERS.

"Now," said the old gentleman, looking at me and laughing, though I saw a tear in his eye, "won't you let them have her?"

"Well, to be sure," said my grandfather. "What can one say after that? Poor things, how pleased they are!"

"Timpey," I said, taking the little girl on my knee, "who do you think is coming to see you? Your mother is coming—coming to see little Timpey!"

The child looked earnestly at me; she evidently had not quite forgotten the name. She opened her blue eyes wider than usual and looked very thoughtful for a minute or two. Then she nodded her head very wisely, and said:

"Dear Mother coming to see Timpey?"

"Bless her!" said the old gentleman, stroking her fair little head; "she seems to know all about it."

Then we sat down to breakfast, and while we were eating it, old Mr. Davis turned to me and asked if I had read the little piece of paper.

"Yes, sir," said my grandfather, "indeed we have read it"; and he told him about Jem Millar, and what he had said to me that last morning. "And now," said my grandfather, "I wish, if you'd be so kind, you would tell me how to get on the Rock, for I'm on sand now; there's no doubt at all about it, and I'm afraid, as you said the last time you were here, that it won't stand the storm."

"It would be a sad thing," said old Mr. Davis, "to be on the sand when the great storm comes."

"Aye, sir, it would," said my grandfather; "I often lie in bed at nights and think of it, when the winds and the waves are raging. I call to mind that verse where it says about the sea and the waves roaring, and men's hearts failing them for fear. Dear me, I should be terribly frightened, that I should, if that day were to come, and I saw the Lord coming in glory."

"But you need not be afraid if you are on the Rock," said our old friend. "All who have come to Christ, and are resting on Him, will feel as safe in that day as you do when there is a storm raging and you are inside this house."

"Yes," said my grandfather, "I see that, sir; but somehow I don't know what you mean by getting on the Rock; I don't quite see it, sir."

"Well," said Mr. Davis, "what would you do if this house were built on the sand down there by the shore, and you knew that the very first storm that came would sweep it away?"

"Do, sir!" said my grandfather. "Why, I should pull it down, every stone of it, and build it up on the rock instead."

"Exactly!" said Mr. Davis. "You have been building your hopes of Heaven on the sand—on your good deeds, on your good intentions, on all sorts of sand heaps. You know you have."

"Yes," said Grandfather, "I know I have."

"Well, my friend," said Mr. Davis, "pull them all down. Say to yourself, 'I'm a lost man if I remain as I am; my hopes are all resting on the sand.' And then build your hopes on something better, something which *will* stand the storm; build them on Christ. He is the only way to Heaven. He has died that you, a poor sinner, might go there. Build your hopes on Him, my friend. Trust in what He has done for you as your only hope of Heaven—*that* is building on the Rock!"

"I see, sir; I understand you now."

"Do that," said Mr. Davis, "and then your hope will be a sure and steadfast hope, a good hope which can never be moved. And when the last great storm comes, it will not touch you; you will be as certainly and as entirely safe in that day as you are in this lighthouse when the storm is raging outside, because you will be built upon the immovable Rock."

I cannot recollect all the conversation which Mr. Davis and my grandfather had that morning, but I do remember that before he went away he knelt down with us and prayed

---

recollect: remember

that we might every one of us be found on the Rock in that last great storm.

And I remember also that that night, when my grandfather said good night to me, he said, "Alick, my lad, I don't mean to go to sleep tonight till I can say, like poor Jem Millar:

> On Christ, the solid Rock, I stand;
> All other ground is sinking sand."

"I want to say that for myself tonight, too," I said. And before long we were both able to say those words truthfully.

CHAPTER 12

The Sunbeam Claimed

It was a cold, cheerless morning; the wind was blowing, and the rain was beating against the windows. It was far too wet and stormy for little Timpey to be out, so she and I had a game of ball together in the kitchen while my father and grandfather went down to the pier.

She looked such a pretty little thing that morning. She had on a clean white pinafore

---

pinafore: a sleeveless apronlike garment worn over a dress

86

and a little blue frock which Mrs. Millar had made for her before she left the island, from cloth my grandfather had bought. She was screaming with delight as I threw the ball over her head and she ran to catch it, when the door opened and my father ran in.

"Alick, is she here? They've come!"

"Who've come, Father?" I said.

"Little Timpey's father and mother; they are coming up the garden now with your grandfather!"

He had hardly finished speaking before my grandfather came in with a lady and gentleman. The lady ran forward as soon as she saw her child, put her arms round her, and held her tightly to her, as if she could never part from her again. Then she sat down with her little darling on her knee, stroking her tiny hands and talking to her, and looking, oh, so anxiously, to see if the child remembered her!

At first Timpey looked a little shy, and hung down her head, and would not look into her mother's face. But this was only for a

---

frock: a dress

minute. As soon as her mother *spoke* to her, she evidently remembered her voice. Mrs. Villiers asked her, with tears in her eyes:

"Do you know me, little Timpey? My dear little Timpey, who am I?"

The child looked up and smiled as she said, "Dear Mother—Timpey's dear mother!" and she put up her little fat hand to stroke her mother's face.

And then when I saw that, I could feel no longer sorry that the child was going away.

I can well remember what a happy morning that was. Mr. and Mrs. Villiers were so kind to us and so very grateful for all that my grandfather and I had done for their little girl. They thought her looking so much better and stronger than when she left India, and they were so pleased to find that she had not forgotten all the little lessons she had learned at home. Mrs. Villiers seemed as if she could not take her eyes off the child; wherever little Timpey went and whatever she was doing, her mother followed her, and I shall never forget how happy and how glad both the father and the mother looked.

But the pleasantest day will come to an end, and in the evening a boat was to come from shore to take Mr. and Mrs. Villiers and their child away.

"Dear me!" said my grandfather with a groan as he took the little girl on his knee. "I never felt so sorry to lose anybody, *never;* I'm sure I didn't. Why, I call her my little sunbeam, sir! You'll excuse me saying so, but I don't feel over and above kindly to you for taking her away from me; I don't indeed, sir."

"Then I don't know what you will say to me when you hear I want to rob you further," said Mr. Villiers.

"Rob me further?" repeated my grandfather.

"Yes," said Mr. Villiers, putting his hand on my shoulder. "I want to take this grandson of yours away too. It seems to me a great pity that such a fine lad should waste his days shut up on this little island. Let him come with me, and I will send him to a really good school for three or four years, and then I will get him some good clerkship, or something of that kind, and put him in the way of making

Saved at Sea

his way in the world. Now then, my friend, will you and his father spare him?"

"Well," said my grandfather, "I don't know what to say to you, sir; it's very good of you—very good, indeed it is—and it would be a fine thing for Alick, it would indeed; but I always thought he would take my place here when I was dead."

"Yes," said my father; "but you see *I* shall be here to do that, Father; and if Mr. Villiers is so very kind as to take Alick, I'm sure we ought only to be too glad for him to have such a friend."

"You're right, David; yes, you're right. We mustn't be selfish, sir; and you'd let him come and see us sometimes, wouldn't you?"

"Oh, to be sure," said Mr. Villiers; "he can come and spend his holidays here and give you fine stories of his school life. Now, Alick, what do you say? There's a capital school in the town where we are going to live, so you would be near us and you could come to see us on holiday afternoons and see whether this little woman remembers all you have taught her. What do you say?"

I was very pleased indeed, and very thankful for his kindness, and my father and grandfather said they would never be able to repay him.

"Repay *me!*" said Mr. Villiers. "Why, my friends, it's *I* who can never repay *you*. Just think for one moment of what you have given me"—and he put his arm round his little girl's neck. "So we may consider that matter settled. And now, when can Alick come?"

My grandfather begged for another month, and Mr. Villiers said that would do very well, as in that time the school would reopen after the holidays. And so it came to pass, that when I said good-bye to little Timpey that afternoon, it was with the hope of soon seeing her again.

Her father called her Lucy, which I found

was her real name. Timpey was a pet name which had been given her as a baby. But though Lucy was certainly a prettier name, still I felt I should always think of her as Timpey—*my* little Timpey.

I shall never forget my feelings that month. A strange new life was opening before me, and I felt quite bewildered by the prospect.

My grandfather and father and I sat over the watch-room fire night after night talking over my future, and day after day I wandered over our dear little island, wondering how I should feel when I said good-bye to it and went into the great world beyond.

Since old Mr. Davis's visit, there had been a great change in our little home. The great Bible had been taken down from its place and carefully read and studied, and Sunday was no longer spent like any other day, but was kept as well as it could be on that lonely island.

My grandfather, I felt sure, was a new man. Old things had passed away; all things had become new. He was dearer to me than ever, and I felt sorrowful when I thought of parting from him.

"I could never leave you, Grandfather," I said one day, "if my father had not been here."

"No," he said, "I don't think I could have spared you, Alick; but your father just came back in the right time—didn't you, David?"

At last the day arrived on which Mr. Villiers had appointed to meet me at the town to which the steamer went every Monday morning when it left the island. My father and grandfather walked with me down to the pier and saw me on board. And the very last thing my grandfather said to me was, "Alick, my lad, keep on the Rock—be sure you keep on the Rock!"

Saved at Sea